# ANTHOLOGY OF
# TRAGEDIES & TRIUMPHS

### EDITED BY

### DON HART
### BOB MACKENZIE
### SHULAMIT ADLER (POETRY)

Production and design by Four Cats Publishing, LLC

*Cover photographs by Ryan Foreman, used by permission*
*Cover design by Tonya Foreman*

ISBN-13: 978-0988839915
ISBN-10: 0988839911

Also by University of Dayton Writers' Group:

*Anthology of Christmas Memories*

# TABLE OF CONTENTS

*Acknowledgments*                                        vii

*Foreword*                                               ix

*Preface*                                                xi

*The Bus Ride* (short story)                             1
by Bob Mackenzie

*Listen to Your Yardstick* (memoir)                      11
by Trillion Smith

*Life's Watershed* (memoir)                              17
by Mollie Kane

*An Unfinished Life* (poem)                              21
by Rosie Huart

*Sugar's Home Now* (memoir)                              23
by Faye Duncan

*Surprise Baby* (memoir)                                 27
by Martha Willis

*I Think You—Therefore You Are* (poem)                   31
by Rosie Huart

*Old Dogs* (memoir)                                      33
by Priscilla Mutter

*The End Is Near, Mom* (poem)                            35
by Bob (Hutch) O'Connor

*Night Thoughts of My Dad* (poem)                        37
by Bob (Hutch) O'Connor

*Four Haikus* (poem)     39
by Ginger Evers

*Life As I Lived It* (memoir)     41
by Donald J. Peacock

*The Golf Game* (memoir)     49
by Rose Peacock

*Baby in the Basket* (short story)     51
by Mary Lou McCarthy

*Then Where?* (poem)     57
by Marianne Woeste

*Solvitur Ambulando* (essay)     59
by Judy Whelley

*Waiting* (poem)     61
by Marian Schwilk-Thomas

*Lady C* (short story)     63
by Wanda Beamer

*The Scrapbook* (short story)     67
by Don Hart

*The Journey* (short story)     75
by Bob Mackenzie

*Patti's Song* (short story)     81
by D. A. Quigley

# ACKNOWLEDGMENTS

Many thanks to the fine people who made this work possible: Bob Mackenzie, Co-editor; Shulamit Adler, Ph.D., Co-editor; Linda Hart, copyediting and formatting; Tonya Foreman, cover design and artwork; Ryan Foreman, cover photography; Nancy Pinard, our Literary Godmother; Don Quigley, Fearless Leader of the Wannabes; Julie Mitchell, Director of Continuing Education, University of Dayton; the fine writers and poets who contributed to this anthology; Four Cats Publishing, LLC; and University of Dayton Osher Lifelong Learning Center, its officers, moderators and staff.

—DON HART, CO-EDITOR

# FOREWORD

It's remarkable how some books come about. Sometimes the story of a book's inception is as curious as the material inside the book. This book, an anthology focusing on tragedies and triumphs in the lives of elderly writers, has this kind of pedigree.

In 2008 a Creative Writing seminar was offered to participants of the University of Dayton Lifelong Learning Institute. We were fortunate when an experienced novelist and instructor, Nancy Pinard, agreed to moderate this seminar. We expected 10 participants and a limited run of enthusiasm. Sixty-five registered!

Since writing can be tough work, we were surprised that such interest was not only sizeable but has been sustained for so long a time (the students organized a writing group and have met monthly for over 6 years). In appreciation, they entitled their moderator henceforth to be known as their "Literary Godmother" and have exchanged hundreds of works among themselves. Two years ago they organized their first collection of works with a holiday theme, *Anthology of Christmas Memories* edited by Don Hart and Bob Mackenzie. It was well received, and I certainly recommend it to you for your Christmas present to yourself this year. It's available online through Amazon or Four Cats Publishing, LLC.

The University of Dayton received endowment funding support for its Lifelong Learning Institute through the Osher Foundation and has been gratefully retitled University of Dayton Osher Lifelong Learning Institute. We are one of 117 Osher Lifelong Learning Institutes across the country, a network dedicated to developing and sharing best practices in the area of senior adult learning. This affiliation has helped our program grow in size and quality so that now senior adults have many more options for expanding their minds and creating friendships with others over 50. We are a community of learners dedicated to sharing our experiences and learning from one another through many fascinating subjects. Creative writing is only one of hundreds of offerings.

The works in this second anthology provide interesting insight available from what you might call "seasoned citizens." Most of the contributors bring more than 70 years of understanding to their writing table. This shows up in the stories presented. I know that you will find the reflections enjoyable.

The writers' group members who contributed to this anthology are all part of our community of lifelong learners at the University of Dayton. They originally called themselves The Wannabes, but based on their achievements since forming this association, the name no longer seems fitting. Members of this group have published dozens of pieces in local publications and no less than five books. What an outstanding accomplishment! I congratulate them all on this dream realized and wish them continued success as committed writers for years to come.

—JULIE MITCHELL

*Julie Mitchell is the Director of Special Programs & Continuing Education and Graduate Academic Affairs at the University of Dayton.*

# PREFACE

It was one of America's great film actresses who said it: "Old age ain't no place for sissies." Bette Davis (1908-1989) gave us this immortal line. She was the perfect messenger for an aphorism like this; her life's theme, on and off camera, was triumph over adversity. She was the sardonic one, willing to take on "cussed roles" other Hollywood women avoided.

When our writing group, made up of members of University of Dayton's Osher Lifelong Learning Institute, was considering a theme for our second anthology, "old age" was one of the choices. After all, you have to be at least 50 years old to join our group, and most of our members are way over that, on average 70 plus. Don Barrett, a creative member who served in World War II, is fond of saying, "Old age ain't for sissies." Most of us thought this was another one of his "originals" until someone pointed out that Bette Davis beat him to it. No matter. We liked the idea and voted to choose this as our theme.

Useful thing about having a lot of mileage behind you is the "experience" you get from making multiple mistakes, which *may* lead to "wisdom," which *may* lead to avoiding mistakes the next time. Notice this is tentative. If you don't learn the right things from the mistakes you've made, "wisdom" eludes you, and you foolishly make 'em again! Added to that is another famous Bette Davis axiom about seniors, "If it works, it probably hurts."

Surrounded as we are with pseudo-wisdom, real experience and time on our hands, older people are likely to have a *few good stories* to tell. In fact, there is a general belief, often unexpressed, that *stories* are critical to human survival. From out of the Stone Age and as recently as last week, we learn from *good stories* what to do and what not to do if we plan to hunt down a mastodon or smoke marijuana. A well-placed anecdote can save us hours of time, thousands of dollars and plenty of embarrassment. So, besides the great entertainment good stories provide, those of us who are more attuned to our survival as we age, we seniors have a built-in gift. We like providing our families and friends with lore that helps them live safely and abundantly.

We hope the stories provided herein give you more insight and enjoyment, whether you are nine or 109. Who knows, your survival might depend on it.

If that doesn't do the trick, or if you crave more of our stuff, check out our first work *Anthology of Christmas Memories* (2011) available through Amazon or our members.

—DON HART, CO-EDITOR

# THE BUS RIDE
## BY BOB MACKENZIE

H arry walked down the lane from his old gray farmhouse past the red barn boasting a faded *Mail Pouch Tobacco* sign, to the two-lane road that ran in front of his place. Here it was Thursday and he had walked down that lane each day this week to catch the bus. But no bus came. And so he struggled back up the lane to wait for another day.

Harry decided that if the bus didn't come tomorrow, he would give it up and not try again. Damn how he wanted that bus to come. How he wanted to take a journey. He thought of it as a road trip, perhaps his last. Harry was old. He felt old. He looked old. It was time for a last trip.

Harry had lived alone for a long time. His wife of 56 years had died some nine years ago, and he still missed her. Ever since then, he had lived alone, though his daughter arrived unexpectedly a short time ago, saying she had come to take care of him.

"Helen, I don't need anyone to take care of me. I have taken care of myself since I was 10, and I've taken care of your mother and you kids forever. I can take care of myself. You should go home and live your own life."

Helen was an odd girl. She had lots of good qualities that enabled her to have a very successful career in office management. She was efficient and a hard worker. However, she just didn't seem to be able to hold onto a guy. Two failed marriages and several affairs left her scarred. Harry couldn't understand her problems with guys, since his marriage had been such a success, and his wife, Jean, had such a good rapport with Helen. Since her first divorce, he often wondered if he had somehow done something wrong. Been a bad example or something. Or maybe Helen was just too bossy. "Hmm," he thought, "office management, perhaps too bossy."

When he got back to the house he felt tired and disappointed, so he bypassed the couch and decided to nap on his bed, the bed he had shared for so long with Jean. Almost immediately his son, Danny, stuck his head in the room to check him.

"You ok, Dad?"

"Yes, Danny, just very tired."

That was another thing. What the hell was Danny doing here? He arrived a day or so ago. Harry worried, "Is this some sort of plot? Are they going to put me in a nursing home? Well that'll be the day. No one is putting me anywhere. I'll go where I please. And they better not try to stop me from doing my road trip either. I need to go to reinvigorate myself. I'll need to catch that bus tomorrow."

For a while Harry thought about Danny. In his way of thinking, Danny was really the successful one, a Wall Street banker, no less, with a trophy wife, three children, and all the toys money could provide. Harry thought, "Man, how I love those grandchildren and great grandchildren." Then, he fell asleep.

Friday morning dawned bright and balmy. The sky was a deep blue, and the sun was glistening. "What a day," Harry thought. "I better get down there and catch the bus."

Once again, Harry walked down the lane and waited by the road. It felt so good to have the sun on his back. He thought about taking his jacket off, but worried about a chill and maybe a cold. "Better to stay covered," he thought.

As he looked to his left down the road he could see something coming, shimmering in the sun. "Is that the bus?" he wondered, "Oh, let it be the bus." Sure enough, as the object got closer, he could make out that indeed it was a bus. As it approached, he waved his arms to signal for the driver to stop.

The doors opened and Harry struggled up the first big step and wondered why the bus didn't have one of those gizmos to lower the front end and make boarding easier. The bus driver greeted Harry with a big smile. He seemed a nice fellow, a bit chubby, but with a bubbly smile that was disarming. Harry smiled back, happy to be beginning his journey. He looked the driver in the face and uttered a line that he had used with many drivers before, "Is this the bus that's taking me to where I'm going?"

"Yes it is," the driver responded with a chuckle. "Grab a seat and we'll be on our way."

Harry looked down the aisle at the half-full bus. Perhaps he would know someone and have a chance to chat. That's when he spotted her, "Oh, surely not," he thought, "not Sarah." The woman he spotted so resembled his first real love that he couldn't take his eyes off her. Oh, how he cared for her back in college and how his heart was broken when she disappeared without a word. It took him a long time to get over her, though he never did forget about her and their time together.

Harry was deep in thought when he heard her speak, "Harry, is that you?"

Her voice hung in his ears, and his heart did a flip; Harry was flabbergasted. "Sarah, is that really you?"

"I'm afraid so, Harry. Why don't you come sit next to me? We can have a nice long chat and reminisce. It will be good to catch up."

Harry sat next to her and the bus began to move. "What are you doing here?" Harry said with utter amazement.

"I'm going on a journey like you."

"This is such a great surprise. I haven't seen you since college," Harry said with a bit of sadness in his voice. It was like the light went out in his eyes.

"Yes, it has been a good long time."

Harry could feel his face growing red with embarrassment, "I shouldn't be saying this after just meeting again, but you know you were my first great love. We had such a good thing together, such good times. It really hurt when you left. For years I wondered why, what happened, did I do something wrong? I had a whole lot of pain and confusion." Harry blushed even more and wished he had kept his mouth shut.

Sarah paused before responding, "Yes, Harry, it was really painful for me too. I'm so, so sorry. At the time I felt that I had no choice. It…it was a family thing. It had nothing to do with you. My father would not allow his Jewish daughter to marry a Catholic. He had such a strong hold over me. I…I don't know, it was all so confusing. I was trying to be a good daughter, obey the commandments, you know, not disobey my father. And, Father was moving the family to Chicago to take a new job. I guess I took the easy road; I acquiesced and went along. I'm sorry I didn't continue to write to you back then: it seemed better to just leave it alone than to continue to work at something I then thought could never be. I guess I was a coward for not standing up to my father and staying in college with you. Please forgive me. I've done my penance, spending countless nights crying, wishing I had the courage to run back to you."

"No, no, that's ok. I'm just glad to have some closure on what happened. Perhaps, now, we can get to know each other again." Harry seemed to brighten up again. "Have you had a good life? Did you ever marry? Any children?"

"Yes, and yes. I did marry, but it was some years after our time together. His name was Ben, a good Jewish man. He was such a good provider and such a good husband and father. We had three children; the youngest, Isaiah, died at the age of three. A car accident. Ben was taking him to the doctor for his checkup when he was broadsided by a truck that ran a red light. They were both killed." Sarah paused for a long time and then continued, "Sometimes I think it was a blessing that Ben died at the same time. He so loved Isaiah;

he would have suffered terribly over his death. I doubt that he would ever have gotten over it, ever healed."

Harry and Sarah remained silent for a long time. Then Sarah said. "What about you Harry, did you ever marry?"

"I'm sorry about your son, how sad." Harry paused for a moment, continuing to feel her pain, and then he went on, "I married a fine young lady named Jean, and we had two children, a son and a daughter. Which reminds me, right now they're both at my house. My daughter, Helen, came to visit me a short time ago and my son arrived in the last few days. I don't get it. Surely I told them I was going on this journey. I suspect they will be upset when they find that I'm gone."

"I suppose they will," Sarah replied, "But they'll get over it. They'll know it's best that you go. You're not a spring chicken anymore." Sarah gave Harry a warm smile, and Harry soaked it up like a sponge. It had been a long time since he had had such an open conversation with a woman.

"Oh my," he wondered, "Would Jean be angry if she knew I was talking to another woman, my first real love?" He hoped not. Then he caught himself. How silly that seemed. Jean had been dead for a long time, and why would she care?

As the bus lumbered along, it dawned on Harry that he had no clear picture of where he was going. No itinerary, and, oh my gosh, no luggage. Suddenly, it all seemed very strange. During all those trips down the lane to look for the bus, he had never questioned where he was going, where he would stay during the trip, or what clothes to pack. He thought, "Darn, I haven't even taken my digital camera. What was I thinking?"

He looked at Sarah. She seemed so serene and self-assured. He was about to speak, when the bus slowed and stopped and two new passengers climbed on board. He studied them carefully, but, no, he didn't know them. They

5

took seats together and began to talk. Harry could not make out what they were saying, but they were obviously excited. Perhaps this was their first journey together for some time. The bus moved on.

Harry shifted his attention back to Sarah. Trying to appear nonchalant, he said, "So, Sarah, where are you going?"

She gave him a strange look, "What do you mean?"

Harry was embarrassed and it showed all over his face. "I...I have a confession to make, I wonder if I'm getting senile. All of a sudden, I realize I don't know where I'm going, and I didn't pack anything for the trip, not even my camera. I never go on a trip without my camera. Suddenly this all seems so strange."

"Oh, Harry, you don't know, do you?"

"Know what, Sarah?"

"Oh my, oh my. I thought you had figured it out. Actually, I thought we all knew."

"All who? What in God's name do you mean?"

"All of us on the bus. Harry, this is our final journey. And, oh, you are going to be so happy when we get where we're going. This is it, Harry; you have been such a good man, such a good husband, and such a good father. You're on that final journey to your great reward."

"Are you saying that I'm dead? How can this be? You're dead too? I don't understand why we're on this bus together? I don't understand anything."

"Oh, Harry, I'm so sorry, but I'm afraid it's true. We're both dead. I wish there was an easier way to say it. And, to answer your question, we're together because it was important to me that you know what happened between us. I wanted you to know why I left and how much I truly loved you."

Harry began to sob. He put his head on Sarah's shoulder and she put her arm around him. "Oh my God, I'm dead, what will my children do? I don't know what to do."

"There is nothing to do, Harry. Your children are all grown now; they'll be fine. They'll be sad for a time, but they have their own lives to live, and they'll live them, just as you and I lived ours. Be calm now, Harry, we'll go through this together, and, believe me, things will be fine."

Harry continued to sob softly. Finally, he lifted his head. He looked so sad that Sarah felt a great pain in her heart for him. "Harry," she said, "tell me what you're thinking. What is making you so sad?"

"I'm thinking about my great grandchildren. So little time. They love their Grandpa and I sure love them. What will they do?"

"They'll be sad for a time just like everyone else who loved you, but you know how resilient young children are. They'll get through it in time. They'll continue to remember you and your love for them. And, Harry, you are not going to lose track of them. Do this for me. Close your eyes and picture the little ones."

Sensing that Harry was going to object, she continued, "No, no, do it please, just try it for a moment."

Harry did try it, and after a few moments, Sarah saw the faint beginnings of a smile at the corner of his mouth. "What do you see?" she whispered.

"I can see them. I can see them! They're playing in their yard, and the dog is running around with them. Their mother is sitting at the picnic table snapping beans. I don't believe it!"

"That's the way it's going to be. You're going to be able to look over them."

"And, what about my children?"

7

"Try it, Harry. Close your eyes again."

"Oh my, they're sitting at the breakfast table crying. I guess they discovered that I'm dead." Harry let out a small anguished cry. Indeed, he could see Helen and Danny. Danny was holding Helen's hand and speaking softly through his tears.

"Helen, we know he's in a better place," said Danny. He hasn't been well for the last six months, and last week, when the doctor recommended Hospice, we knew it wouldn't be long. I hated seeing him lie in that bed all week. I know the nurses took good care and made him as comfortable as possible, but, in a way, it was like he had already gone."

"What are we going to do without him, Danny? I'm going to miss him terribly."

"We're going to grieve for him just like we did when Mom died. We're both strong people thanks to all the things our parents taught us." After a long pause Danny continued, "Dad was a good man. I'm sure he's gone to a good reward. He taught us well. We'll be ok. And I'm sure that he'll be watching over us."

Danny stood up, took Sarah's hand, and guided her out of her chair. He pulled her to himself and hugged her. They both began to sob again. After a long while, Danny said through his sobs, "We were lucky to have had him for so long. He taught us well."

Helen looked at him though her tears, "Yes, our lives will go on. And I'm sure you're right. Dad will be looking over us."

Harry opened his eyes and looked at Helen. All the stress and grief seemed to have evaporated from his face. "Sarah, I think they're going to be ok. Everyone's going to be ok." He took Sarah's hand and smiled, "Let's get on with this journey; it's time to see Jean, and Ben and Isaiah."

Sarah smiled as she looked into Harry's now calm face, "I bet they'll be waiting to greet us when we get off the bus."

*In this story, Don Hart writes under his pen name, Trillion Smith. This story will be included in his forthcoming personal anthology titled The Adventures of Trillion Smith.*

# LISTEN TO YOUR YARDSTICK
## BY TRILLION SMITH

I t was 1949 when I first got "persuaded" in Catholic grade school by the intrepid Sister Dominica. She hit me with a long ruler on the left side of my arm, just above the elbow. It hurt like blazes. The girls in my class found out her civilian name was Joan Yardley and she came from Stickston, Texas. The kids all called her "Sister Mary Yardstick." She turned out to be the best teacher I ever had, better in many ways than professors who taught me post-graduate courses.

The reason for my "persuasion" was that I "would not *listen*." I wanted to talk instead. Poor Yardstick was trying to teach 46 children in fourth grade. Her philosophy was "no discipline, no learning." She was dead right on that count. Nowadays her discipline would land her a prison sentence of 10 years to life, but those were different days. And kids, though rebellious as always, acquired ethical training and good sense when the rod was *not* spared. For example, my parents backed up Sister Yardstick 100%, no questions asked. When my mother found out the formidable sister left a visible "persuasion mark" on my left arm, she applied a similar mark on my right arm at home "just to balance things out."

Yardstick taught me three good lessons: How to Really Listen, How to Spell and How to Deal Skillfully with Authority. All three of these talents gave me critical advantages in a long life. Especially, learning to listen expertly while pretending not to hear a damn thing! General Charles DeGaulle, a president of France who was famous for this trait, could not have learned it from a better source. The sister did not bother to separate lessons and instead

11

combined them into an unforgettable exercise. It all started with Miss Pell, who was an imaginary person.

Whenever a kid spelled a word wrong, as in "misspell," he was promptly "sent to Miss Pell." She supposedly stood outside our classroom door (but invisible to children under 19). Sister Mary Yardstick, 36-inch ruler in hand, ordered you to pick up an enormous green dictionary from the corner of her desk, carry it out to a table in the hall, open the huge tome and "consult Miss Pell." This imaginary Spelling Teacher never talked and never appeared. Your ridiculous mission was to go through that gigantic book and find (with Pell's advice) how to correctly spell the word by "sounding it out." Impossible! If you knew how to spell it, would you need an 18-pound dictionary!? If you did not know, how would you look it up? The ever-present yardstick focused your attention. (You did not goof off in the hall, either.) The dilemma made Catch 22 seem rather easy.

One time, the *Word of the Day* was "listen." Notice the "t" in that word? I knew how to spell it alright, but I told Yardstick it should be spelled "lis-sun." I also told her 50 visits to Miss Pell would not change my opinion. The kids laughed out loud in total agreement. Weren't we supposed to "sound it out?" Nearly all of my friends had been trapped by silent letters. "If you really didn't know the right way to spell gnat," I told her, "you could be stuck in the hall for 4-½ years waiting for a hint from Miss Pell." More laughter.

Then a few kids came to my rescue. "Why do we spell know with a 'k' and a 'w?' It should be spelt 'n-o.' Why is that 'h' in school? Nobody ever "huffs" it. Words like dog and cat are good, but what's that 'c' doing in the word 'mice?' Shouldn't it be 'mys?' What's the 'gh' doing in rough and tough? Did we run out of 'f's'?"

The world of letters was clearly dysfunctional in our minds; now was a good time to begin to 'strayten' it out! I could feel the authority draining from Sister Yardstick's ruler.

That's when she really came after me! She ordered me to stand at attention in front of her desk and hold out my hands. I could almost feel the ruler coming down on them.

She took out several pieces of lined paper and began writing while I stood there with my hands stretched out. Maybe she was writing a scathing letter to my mother before hitting me on the hands, or maybe I was in for both. What happened was worse.

She kept writing in that excellent "nun penmanship" until she had a whole paragraph filled out, which included my name. Then she began numbering the lines. After she numbered lines up to 50, she stapled another a few pages together, stood and put her yardstick into my outstretched hands and directed me to sit in her chair and lay the sacred stick on her desktop. She quietly ordered me to keep numbering lines until I got up to 200.

The kids got a huge laugh out of me sitting in her chair, yardstick on her desk "at the ready," while I sat there writing. She was standing at attention in the front of the desk now, hands outstretched, reversing our situations. I never even considered giving *her* a "small shot of persuasion." When I had the numbers done perfectly, she motioned for me to come out in front of the desk and put the pages into her outstretched hands. I had no idea what she had written on the first page, but it wasn't long till I knew. She pointed to the first word on the page and ordered me to write it *big* on the backboard.

The word was PETITION. I thought it had something to do with dogs and cats, since the first part of the word began with pet... She opened her 18-pound dictionary almost immediately to that word and made me read the definition to the class. I read it out loud, but I didn't understand a darn thing of what I read. Over the next two weeks, however, I became an expert on the term.

Yardstick announced to the class that I needed to collect 200 adult signatures on that petition, and as soon as I got them she would allow all her students to henceforth spell the word "lis-sun." Everyone cheered, including me. I had two weeks to get those signatures—piece of cake.

PETITION

BE IT RESOLVED THAT HENCEFORTH THE ENGLISH WORD "listen" BE SPELLED "lissun," INASMUCH AS IT SOUNDS PHONETICALLY CORRECT AND IS EASIER FOR CHILDREN TO SPELL.

I HEREBY AGREE THAT BY AFFIXING MY SIGNATURE HEREON I APPROVE THAT TRILLION SMITH AND HIS GRADESCHOOL CLASSMATES, PROVIDING THAT SUFFICIENT ADULTS CONCUR, WOULD HEREBY BE PERMITTED TO SPELL THIS WORD AS MODIFIED ABOVE.

That same afternoon, when school had been out several hours, my petition project began to unravel. Mr. and Mrs. Kroboffsky, my nice foreign neighbors, were pleased to sign my petition. So was my Aunt Betty, who was only a few years older than me. My dad and mother, and all of my adult neighbors, laughed in my face. Adults on my paper route laughed too. None of them would sign the petition except Mr. Maloney, who was drinking beer on his porch. His wife scolded him for doing it. I did not understand why, since she was so nice to me otherwise. He laughed too, just like the others. He asked me if I would show him the petition again, once I got the rest of the signatures. I never showed it to him again.

I was beginning to think it would have been better if the nun had hit me with her stick, rather than let me face this ridicule.

My aunts and uncles wouldn't sign either, and these were the adults I was really counting on. Some of them would have died for me, but sign a simple petition for me… no way. This was getting embarrassing. All the adults in my neighborhood seemed to know about that petition before I asked them.

They knew I was right, too, but they just wouldn't help me.

The old policeman who lived nearby was good friends with my priest. They both liked me and sometimes we'd go fishing together. They wouldn't sign the petition either. Both of them said I was headed for serious trouble trying to stand up to the Sister this way. The retired professor, who let me cut his grass for $1.50, told me he'd "rather sign a bad check." I didn't understand at all when he said I was fighting a thousand years of the King's English. Didn't we get completely away from that English king? Wasn't America a democracy?

I wound up with a total of seven signatures. I was only 193 short. My beautiful Aunt Betty's signature was probably questionable, since she was only 15, but looked 23. Over the years, hundreds of people have asked me about that petition.

Yardstick won a decisive victory back then, which she could not have done if she had all the free rulers from the lumberyard. I pray that she and her stick will some day be with God in heaven, but I also wish she were beside us now to protect our language from all its new abuses.

For me, the word "listen" became more than just hearing. When I was old enough to understand, the retired professor explained that the word was derived from an older meaning for 'lust,' as in the lustiness of a baby's cry, or a child's lust for learning. From then on, reluctantly, I've been going along with that 't' in LISTEN.

*Effort of overcoming adversity is a watershed in memory. The 1913 Dayton, Ohio Flood divided Mollie Kane's family reminiscences for near a century in only one of two ways. Thus, memories of the past began "Before the Flood" or "After the Flood." Mollie Kane is a nom de plume for Cindy Keefer.*

# LIFE'S WATERSHED
## BY MOLLIE KANE

M y grandfather carried a military spine out of the Civil War, and he walked behind a long pointed beard that swayed the width of his suspenders. Grandfather maintained his independence with a few coins by walking a paper route well into this, his sixty-fifth year. Papa, his only child, was a letter carrier. Every morning Grandfather returned from his circuit just as Papa finished his breakfast tea, daily mush and morning newspaper. You could set a clock to the opening of the door and the following question, "How's the mush?"

Mama tightened her jaw. She knew her mush was perfect. My grandmother died shortly after Papa's birth. Papa married late in life, and he and his father lived as bachelors for some forty odd years. The thought that two men would question Mama's cooking galled her.

The day the door opened, when Grandfather entered, stomped the slush off his shoes and silently sank into his chair, was our watershed. Papa's head bolted up from his teacup and Mama froze at the cook stove, her wooden stir-spoon stopped in mid air. "You better not go to work," Grandfather whispered in a shaky voice. "The levee is going to break. I saw boxcars floating on the river. If those cars breach the river's path, their power will knock our house off its foundation."

What does it mean, "If they breach the river's path? Who is they?"

Papa nodded. It was expected. For days, it had rained, sleeted and now snowflakes fell. Mama called out orders to us three children as she gathered candles and matches. Grandfather ate his mush and then went into the backyard and returned with our laying hens. I pushed our beagle up the stairs. He resisted me as much as a condemned man climbing the steps of the guillotine. I'm sure he thought he was going to his death since he had lived a life of whacks when he tried to follow us children upstairs. Papa carried Mama's market basket filled with crackers, jam and a fresh loaf of bread. From the second floor, Grandfather opened the attic door and we ascended. When we were settled for our wait, Papa returned to the first floor staircase. He closed the French doors that rested halfway up the steps on a landing where I liked to play elevator, opening and closing the doors for my siblings.

In quietude, our family settled in and then pressed our faces to the many windows of our attic. Mama cried out and our heads turned from the rising water. With her hand to her opened mouth she sobbed, "Mr. Turner, I forgot water!" Papa quickly moved to her side and took her in his arms. Stunned, we children stared at our Victorian parents. Never had we seen them in a public display of affection. Papa rubbed her back to our horror. Then we knew we were going to die. Fear coiled around our hearts and turned our teeth to clattering. Oh my Lord, Papa kissed her cheek and said, "Mrs. Turner, it is too dangerous for you to return. Oh Lord," Papa's words sank away as he whispered in her ear. His lips touched her delicate skin. We turned our heads quickly away from their moment. My sister swooned. Then we knew it was really a bad situation because Papa kissed Mama.

Noise of a rattling wagon sent everyone back to the windows. A family was passing our house in a wagon. The woman held a baby in her arms as she sat on the bench with her husband. Children and furnishings filled the wagon bed. Mama flung open a window, "Please come in." Mama begged. "You'll never make it." The woman in the wagon turned pitiful eyes up toward our attic, while the man vehemently shook his head and continued to whip his white, mouth-foaming horse. Just then the levee broke and we watched the wagon being pushed over, dumping its contents into floodwater eddies full of dead horses and braying mules; never did the family surface for one last breath of air.

A loud knocking directed out attention in a different direction. Mama believed it was the front door. "It is not locked," she called.

Papa pulled her down beside him. "It is only the piano knocking into the ceiling, Mrs. Turner." Tears filled her eyes. Mama had saved her egg money to purchase the monster below. She was proud she had never cut into Papa's salary. I was happy the monster, which held me in hours of excruciating lessons, was wounded, maybe never to be played again, and I turned my smile away from Mama.

Fires burned on the city's south side. We watched them throw flame ribbons against the black sky throughout the night. Dawn broke and we could see men rowing a boat toward our attic window. We were offered a ride and Papa accepted. My poor sweet Mama hiked up her petticoat and skirt and stepped over the windowsill into the boat. I stared dumbly. I had never seen a naked part of her body except her hands and her arms when she rolled up her shirtsleeves on wash day. Face does not count. Mama showed the boatmen her ankle and gam.

Floodwater swirled maddeningly while the men steadied the boat against the house as we climbed in. Jubilantly. I trailed my fingers in the water. Mama screamed, "Do you think you are at a picnic?" I yanked my hand inside the boat. Mama had never screeched in my life, but then Mama could not swim. Papa patted her back. Oh Lord, not in front of these outside rescuers. I turned crimson and wished myself anyplace but in this boat.

19

*A young friend of the author's asked her to write his eulogy and later chose to end his life. He was technically very gifted. However, he was also very misunderstood in life. The author gave this poem a voice in hope that others might see beyond a human and limited perspective.*

## AN UNFINISHED LIFE
### BY ROSIE HUART

My heart is heavy and in tears.
Are there others who sing your song?
Praising courage. Dispelling fears.
Blinded souls cry out, "What went wrong?"

And stone casters throw projected shame
In pretending to be right and strong.
Blessed are those who revere your name.
Creative beauty in disguise
Honoring you from where you came.

I loved looking into your eyes
Imaging a soul born of grace
Spreading wings and eager to fly.
The heavens call for your embrace.
Leaving behind cages that bind.
Singing joy from another place.
Farewell, dear artist friend, of mine.
Cherished hearts need no explanation.
Bravery is what you leave behind.

My heart is heavy and in tears.
Praising courage. Dispelling fears.

*This work is in tribute to the author's dear friend and neighbor Berthe Weist. It appears in the author's poetry and memoir collection titled Seasons of Life: A Journey Within, published in 2013.*

## SUGAR'S HOME NOW
### BY FAYE DUNCAN

That January day dawned with temperatures far below normal and continued to plummet to near zero. Snow had been plowed into miniature mountains along the roadside. I was, however, quite warm in my oven-heated kitchen, preparing dinner, when my longtime neighbor opened the front door, simultaneously calling my name. It surprised me that she entered in such an abrupt way, and I came quickly, drying my hands as I came.

"Is Ron here?" she asked, breathlessly. "No, not at the moment, but he should be here soon," I answered, still puzzling over her unusual behavior.

"Okay," she managed to emit with obvious effort, and turning to leave as quickly as she had come, she added, "I think Sugar Bear is dying and I wanted him to help me get her into the car so I can get her to the vet." Her voice was filled with anxiety, and by the time she finished her explanation, she was off the porch and halfway down the driveway, hurrying back to the big, black dog we had all come to love over the years.

Sugar Bear, that slow, lumbering Labrador retriever, had changed so much since we first met her. Could it have been fourteen years ago that I had watched her romping with my daughter, chasing squirrels from lawn to lawn and up the trees, barking viciously at the postman or any other person that threatened her domain? Would she really bite? I had often questioned. I, too, would not have taken a chance, just as many would not, stopping in their tracks until Berthe had commanded her to "heel".

Once a frisky pup, she was now aged and much over-

23

weight, and I had known instinctively her days were numbered. Lately, she had moved about sluggishly, unaware of much that happened around her.

She had been good for my friend—a companion to make the house alive when Berthe returned from work. I could only imagine how terribly lonely living alone would be. Sugar Bear had filled her life with a friendship I might never understand, for animals were not a necessary part of my existence. I called after her that I would be right there, doubting that she heard me, but before she entered the street, her ample cape flapping in the crisp, winter air, I had donned my coat, mittens, and boots, pulled the door shut and was following her.

She was a large woman with soft, olive complexion. Her eyes were kindness personified and I truly admired her. I had never known her husband; his death had come prior to our becoming a part of this neighborhood nearly twenty-four years ago. We were friends, I knew, and I would always be grateful for her friendship.

Berthe reached for her knitted cap and pulled it tightly over her ears as she called lovingly to her pet, urging her to struggle to her feet so that she might get into the car of her own volition. Sugar Bear had managed to carry her weakened body through the garage, but could go no further. It was there I first saw her as I turned in front of the car. She was obviously very sick indeed. As together we tried to coax her up, I was soon aware that she was powerless to lift her own feeble body. We would have no choice but to carry her.

How much did she actually weigh? I had no conception —nor had I ever considered it. One hundred pounds? One hundred thirty? But now, her weight was ponderous for she was nearly unconscious. Berthe bent over, placing her hands under Sugar's rear legs and body, while I wrestled to lift her shoulders, feeling utterly helpless as her head dropped backward, her tongue extending languidly as she gasped for breath. She had scarcely any life left, I felt sure, but I could not let my friend suspect my fears.

Struggling to hold her, we took still another step toward the car's rear door. I felt her slipping from our hands as my muscles strained to hold on for a few more feet. Her weight proving to be too much and our grip nearly lost, we lowered her gently to the snow-covered ground. In our attempt to lift her again, I became suddenly very frightened for my friend's well being. All the recent warnings flashed across my mind: the dangers of overexertion, particularly in extreme temperatures and under emotional stress. I had to do something! With a fervent prayer, I asked for added strength to get Sugar into the car so that Berthe might be spared any further strain on her already over-tired and emotionally drained body.

I should not have been surprised, for I believed, didn't I, that I could lift the dead weight of that dying animal because I must do it, and yet, when the strength came so quickly to my overtaxed muscles, I was awed at the realization of answered prayer. The adrenaline in my body had surged to create unusual strength, as God had willed it from the moment of His human creation. My conscious prayer had enacted it. The door closed on my black animal friend, and I knew then that I must now ask that comfort be given to Berthe as she lost her companion.

Nearly an hour and a half later, just as we were finishing dinner, the doorbell chimed. Answering, my son greeted Berthe, and through the door, into the dining room, I heard the rattle of a chain. There they were—my dear friend with tear-stained eyes trying to be brave and nonchalant, and a new friend—large, black, and very much like another I knew. She sniffed and darted, nosing around the kitchen and back to the living room, pulling her leash taut while Berthe introduced us to Brandy.

"It was the only way. I knew I had to bring her home with me," Berthe's voice cracked as I threw my arms around her and held her one brief moment. We knew we understood each other—words really were not necessary.

# SURPRISE BABY
## BY MARTHA WILLIS

"Mom and Dad, are you sitting down? I have some news." It was our son David, age 53, father of three unmarried sons. As Charlie and I responded on our kitchen speakerphone, a fleeting thought ricocheted around my mind that perhaps a pregnancy was involved here. Oh, I'm such a suspicious grandmother! I sat down.

"Well, I just need to tell you that Jamey has gotten his girlfriend, Katie, pregnant and the baby is due in six months." Oh my gosh! My thoughts whirled. It wasn't the oldest son, Andy, age 22, or 20-year-old Sam. No, the deed was done by Jamey, the 14-year-old eighth grade student. Jamey is a sweet and shy boy who loves to "workout" and who since elementary school has developed muscles like a budding body builder. He can run like the wind, bench press a shocking amount, and has done nightly push-ups as regularly as the sun rises.

David divorced the boys' mother, Carol, after 17 years of marriage. All three of David's sons live with him in a small, three-bedroom apartment across town. The boys are all healthy, fun-loving, happy kids who are *not* independent. David works at a fairly well paying job and takes care of them in every way—cooking, cleaning, shopping. He gives them spending money and buys them tons of videos; he generally overindulges them.

Fortunately (or maybe not) for Jamey, his brothers have often included him in their activities. He knew way too much way too early. They had watched lots of war and "other" movies together and been supportive of one another during the divorce. The circumstances of their lives were like glue to their relationships. Carol who is now married to Satan (as the boys describe him) was, and is, the disciplinarian. Thus, the boys had chosen to live with David.

27

They see their mom often but only go to her home when her new husband works second shift.

Upon being told the news of a baby due, Andy, the oldest brother, gave a typical Andy response, "I'm here for you, buddy. Let me know what I can do to help." Andy had a part time job in a retail store and was going to the local community college to become a fireman. Andy is calm and kind and has great people skills. Academics are his challenge, but his skill is in helping others. He is naïve and nice, causing all in the family to look out for him.

Brother Sam is a 20-year-old Marine based in Okinawa, tall with dark brown hair—short back and sides—and snapping brown eyes. He has a wild and crazy sense of humor and a quick temper. He is charming and tough and has always been a mentor for Jamey. "I'm teaching Jamey everything I know," he often said. I cringed every time he said it. The week after graduating from high school, Sam discovered a Marine recruiter, and it was a hand in glove thing from then on. I believe Sam even loved basic training at Parris Island. His comment to Jamey at the news was, "You dumb-ass, I told you to use condoms."

A few months before the dropping of this bomb, Jamey had said to me, "Grandma, you should meet my girlfriend, Katie. She's really hot!" I met Katie soon after. At Jamey's request, we invited her over for one of our many family dinners. And sure enough, Katie was a sexy little blond with great make-up and a mature figure on a small frame. Oh, let the worrying begin.

There had been signs everywhere for a long time that this event could occur. We could have put an ad in the newspaper a year before that a baby would show up about this time in this family. Jamey was torn between both parents, wanting to spend time with each and yet telling me one day that he felt like he just didn't have a place of his own. Katie is from a problem-filled family. She and her little brother are in the custody of her paternal grandmother. The parents fell into the black hole of drug and alcohol abuse causing the children to be ordered by the court to live with the grandmother. Katie was definitely looking for a way out.

The Way Out: Baby Brandon was born in April of last year. His birth was very easy, which is amazing since births to 14-year-olds are considered very high risk. He appeared four hours after labor started. His APGAR score—the evaluating standards assessing the health of a newborn—was the highest possible. He was a full-term baby and weighed just over eight pounds with not a mark on his body; he had beautiful fluffy, yellow chick hair. Mother Katie looked ready to walk home a few hours after the birth. Relatives from every corner of both families visited in the hospital room early. At one point, there were three great grandmothers, a great grandfather, a grandmother, aunts, uncles and friends all in the hospital room. Katie held the baby giving him his first bottle, and Jamey, sitting proudly by them, was emotional. They were just two little kids having a baby, but they had just mastered the major event of twenty- to thirty-year-olds. Lord, this was a day I'll never forget.

There followed life-changing conversations, entanglements, and drama without great damage. The "deciders" in the family chose to keep the baby and not give him up for adoption. These were the parents, grandmother, and the kids who were parents of the baby. There developed involved plans about Brandon's care—where he would stay, by whom he would be cared for, and who would pay what. Amazingly, it had worked out peacefully without acrimony. Carol had led the way in this regard. She is a super negotiator and her career field is early childhood care and education—a great help.

It's been 16 months since Brandon came to us all. He is just a very special baby. Of course, all great grandparents think that. But here is my pure proof, Brandon rarely cries unless he is hurt or hungry. He goes to sleep on his own without being rocked and hums himself to sleep. When he was fed milk from a bottle (which he has recently given up) and ate his first solid food, he cooed with delight and appreciation. He has rarely had any kind of illness and has no allergies or deficits. He walked in good time and is an adventurer—wanting to touch, feel and taste everything. Laughter and giggles are his specialty, and he often teases, flirts and performs in restaurants. He waves and smiles and has an excited look anytime people give him attention. When music reaches his ears, his little hips sway back and forth and he smiles with joy. Brandon sleeps well, eats well, and knows no stranger. I call him an easy baby. He is God's gift to us all. We love him to pieces.

Brandon sleeps in three or four different beds every week. He has a loving babysitter four days a week—a sweet middle-aged lady who cares for him only during the day in her home. My husband and I, two of the many great grandparents, keep him every Sunday through Monday. We have a baby bed in our bedroom. It isn't easy, but in some ways he is keeping us young. He lives with our son, David, along with Katie and Jamey. The now 16-year-old parents take care of him some of the time with supervision, but their school and homework take much time, and still being young teens, they also require parenting. Brandon goes to Grandmother Carol's sometimes on the weekend. His social calendar is filled with great grandparents and other family members taking turns loving and caring for him. Diapers, milk, food and healthcare come from many sources. We're all pitching in. So far, it's working!

If I let my mind wander, I can create many reasons for concern down the road. I find that to be a foolish time-waster. It is now late 2012. I have no control over the future and have decided to save my energy for fun times with Brandon. He is our pride and joy, and we feel so blessed to have lived long enough to know this magnificent great grandson.

*This poem was written a few days after the author's young friend was shot and killed by a member of his family. He was only 22. He was not only a dear friend but was also the author's computer teacher. They met every week for a couple of years and shared stories, food and most of all friendship. Instead of attending his public memorial, the author chose to have her own personal memorial by honoring him with a poem.*

# I THINK YOU—THEREFORE YOU ARE
## BY ROSIE HUART

I paid you homage today.
I went to the garden and found you
in the diamond dew on the wispy fern.

There—you glistened
in the sunlight.
I caught you dancing with butterflies
And doing somersaults in the air.
Throughout the yard

I saw you shimmer.
Even my hand
had your sparkle on it.
I smelled you
in the fragrance surrounding me.

I invited you
into the silence.
I heard you
call my name in the murmur of the crickets and birds.
I think—you.
Therefore, you are.

# OLD DOGS
## BY PRISCILLA MUTTER

It's 8 AM, below freezing, and barely light out when my husband and I bundle ourselves into long johns, warm jackets and knit wool hats. I put on my "dog clothes"—my ancient, fiber-filled jacket and my brown lace-up Lands End snow boots. A crust of ice over snow covers our driveway and the rest of the landscape. We and our Labrador retriever, Emma, walk down the driveway to the street, then left to the path by the river.

We're 81 and 76. When we bought Emma, a 12-week-old puppy, we didn't think of the responsibility to two aging people. Now at 13, she's a muscular, athletic dog, slowing down a little because of stiff joints, but we take her for a walk, twice a day, rain or shine.

We are lucky to live in an urban area with easy access to a river path. In less than three minutes, we can be in a place where there are no signs of human beings except for traffic noise on nearby Interstate 70 and our river path itself, which we and woodland animals and other nature lovers have worn.

Emma wakes us early every morning, reminding us that it's time to get up and get with it. She never tires of checking out the scents of the nocturnal travelers that use our path. She smells raccoons, groundhogs, skunks, foxes, and other dogs. When she finds something important that passed through recently, say, a deer or coyote, her hackles rise, and she bounds ahead of us on the trail, barking and growling. She sniffs a plant stalk for several seconds, motionless except for her twitching black nose.

Because we are out every day, we're attuned to the seasons. We see the seasonal progression of the wildflowers. In early spring, there are creamy white flowers—bloodroot, Dutchman's breeches and anemone. Later in the summer, there are bright blue chicory blossoms and a variety of sunflowers. Fall brings the vibrant purples and golds—ironweed, asters, goldenrod.

We know when and where migratory birds nest and when their young fledge. We watch for our resident turkey vultures perched on the snags of dead trees across the river. We know where we will flush a croaking great blue heron and a chattering kingfisher.

People think we're crazy to drag ourselves out every day, especially in weather extremes. We have a fenced yard, and Emma would get along without her twice-a-day walks. But the dog walks, regardless of their inconvenience and difficulties, have taken on a place of their own in our lives.

They can be inconvenient and uncomfortable, even miserable. In summer, we get soaked to the skin with sweat, thanks to our notorious Midwest heat and humidity. Winters are another thing. I have fallen flat on my back on ice more than once—nothing broken. I attribute this resilience mostly to the daily dog walks.

We get rashes from poison ivy and stinging nettles, get bitten and stung by ticks, chiggers, bees, mosquitoes and wasps. We don't worry about Lyme disease or West Nile. We figure we've caught them by now and are immune.

How long can we continue these walks? We notice our bodies changing. It takes a little longer each morning to work out the stiffness. But not as long as it would take if we didn't go on dog walks. A physician friend said there is research showing that owning a dog extends one's life by about three years. We understand why.

Emma is getting older, grey around her muzzle, stiffer, getting tired a little sooner, especially on hot summer days. We'll keep walking even when she's gone. Our walks benefit us as much if not more than they do Emma.

# THE END IS NEAR, MOM
## BY BOB (HUTCH) O'CONNOR

The long self-assigned minutes slowly,
Oh how amazingly slowly, drift by.
We anxiously, pleadingly bombard heaven
With tear-filled prayers for our wait to end.

But, with an all-knowing God directing
All human's entire earthly journey,
Time is a meaningless measurement
There is no time in eternity!

It is early evening December 8, 1982
In the ICU Unit of Marion General,
And our mom, the sweetest, loving, most gracious
Mother in this world, is close to breathing her last!

Consciously my twin sister and I deny the inevitable,
But subconsciously pray Mom will go quickly
To the warm secure embrace of eternity
Life ebbs away—Mom drifts into coma...

We begin to whisper to her precious memories:
Lazy summer days at Chippewa Lake,
Fun filled family reunions in the Valley,
Lakewood Park, the Costello's, Clarke's & O'Connor's
Family outings at many Ohio State Parks
And finally, we sing the soul-searching melody of
Mom's favorite Hymn, *"GOOD NIGHT SWEET JESUS"!*

GOOD NIGHT, MOM!

Lucille O'Connor
1903-1982

# NIGHT THOUGHTS OF MY DAD
## BY BOB (HUTCH) O'CONNOR

After the shadows of night sleep
And darkness clothes the landscape,
I meditate on today's browsings.
Before consciousness drifts into the deep memories of my past,
I pause.
I express my gratitude to God for today:
For the brilliance of this morning's sunrise,
The uplifting laughter of children
And the spoken love of family and friends;
For the lazy breezes that silently ruffle the trees,
The rabbits, squirrels and birds—all the living creatures
That fascinate our world with movement and song.
For these and the many other tangible enjoyments of my life,
I give unbounded gratitude to our gracious Creator.

Before sleep envelops my tired mind and body,
I set the stage for dreaming.
This night, I search the recesses of my mind for details:
There I am
Just 16—embarking on the long-anticipated trip.
Just Dad and me. No one else to share Dad with!
We are driving leisurely over rural countryside,
Not speaking. Silence increases our awareness of each other.
This is the best of times for father and son.
We stop for the evening on a hill overlooking Lake Erie.
So vivid now: Dad, slowly smoking his daily cigar,
Quietly inhales Nature's awesome beauty.
Again, we commune in silence.

My quiet dad was a tower of loving strength.
He instilled in me his solid values: fairness, the importance of love,
Of God, family and fellow man
And respect for all God's Creation.
I am a much better man today for having this great Dad.
He gave unselfishly of his entire being to all who knew him
To family, friends, co-workers and especially
To me!
Oh, how I miss you, Dad.

In memoriam: Francis H. O'Connor, 1903-1979

# FOUR HAIKUS
## BY GINGER EVERS

**Growing Older**

Courage in old age
Facing challenges with grace
God is on our side!

**Grandparents**

Wrinkles are laugh lines
Grandparents cherish the young
Hugs, kisses and love

**Pain**

Throbbing, aching, pain
Suffering from injury
I know I'm alive!

**Retirement**

Many years of work
Time for friends and family
But where's the money?

# LIFE AS I LIVED IT
## BY DONALD J. PEACOCK

Writing about tragedies and triumphs is very personal. These terms can only be defined by the person living them. A triumph can be as varied as winning a million-dollar lottery or as small as winning a candy bar. It can be as big as surviving an airplane crash or as small as not stubbing your sore toe on something. Likewise, a tragedy for some people can be their whole life, or on the opposite side, a triumph can also represent a person's whole life. For my life the split is toward the triumph side as my tragedies have been minimal.

In our quiet, tranquil family there existed an entity who had a strong impact on me. He had the same characteristics and attitudes I did. When I looked in a mirror, I could have been looking at either one of us. He was my identical twin brother. This, in my mind, was my first triumph.

In 1936, the year we were born, techniques for detecting multiple fetuses were not well developed, so I came as a complete surprise to my parents. I say 'I' because my brother preceded me into the world by ten to fifteen minutes. I think he hogged the nutrients also because our mother told me many times that I was the runt, and they were not sure I would make it. The fact that I am now 76 years old probably represents some kind of triumph, which could have been a tragedy.

I am quite sure that unless someone has a multiple birth sibling they cannot begin to understand the relationship. I think multiple birth siblings who are not identical, such as fraternal twins, do not have the same relationship that we did. Identical twins come from one egg that splits, while non-identical twins come from two separate eggs. It has even been proven that identical twins have identical DNA. We thought alike, acted alike, and usually got into trouble alike. For the first six to seven years, our mother dressed us alike. She eventually found that there was one thing we did not want to do alike. We knew we were individuals, and we wanted others to know that also. She had no problem with this.

I cannot remember doing anything that we did not do together. We even both went to work at Wright-Patterson Air Force Base. My brother, just like our births, preceded me to the base, but by two weeks instead of fifteen minutes. I took a side jaunt to help our father drive a car to Los Angeles, where he had a summer job. My brother had an apartment by the time I got there, so I moved in with him. This apartment was just off Monument Avenue, close to the river. This was an area where you could get an inexpensive apartment. In fact, the young lady who lived across the hall apparently had her own way of earning the rent money. She had many gentlemen callers each evening. We very quickly moved to a top floor apartment in a private home.

After about two years, the laboratory where my brother worked had a cutback, and he was one of the casualties, thus starting our divergence. At the end of the summer, he went back to New Orleans and to graduate school. My triumph was that I retired in 1993, and he had to work until 2001.

As much or as little as we diverged, things remained unchanged. Only distance was a factor, and sometimes not *the* factor. One time we got new glasses at about the same time, and from one thousand miles apart we separately picked out the same frames. Apart we were still a great deal alike and will always remain so. We only talk on the phone every few months. But my wife always knows who I am talking to by the length of the conversation and the uproarious laughs that are generated.

My adulthood life also revolves around one singularly important person. I had been working at Wright-Patterson Air Force Base for about five years, living a reasonably typical single life, involved with in-house research and starting into managing contracts, which guaranteed more promotions and money.

One day as I delivered my time sheet for the week to the front office, I saw that a new secretary had reported in. I spoke, we chatted a while and then I went back to work. Then I came back and chatted some more, and then later, I came back and chatted more. After a time of chatting, I worked up courage enough to asked her if she would go to the movies with me. She hesitated for a while and finally said yes. To make a short story long, we dated for about a year, and then one day, while sitting in my car in the parking lot of a small restaurant I asked her to marry me. Even with all of my sterling qualities, she had to think about it for a while. Finally, she decided that I met her requirements, among those probably was "being trainable," which I could not deny needing, and so, she said yes. The marriage has lasted forty-eight years as of May 15, 2013. This I consider a major triumph in my life.

The impact of the arts on my life has been, generally, to improve it. This combined with my many hobbies, past to present, has greatly improved my enjoyment of life. But as with any bunch of roses, there is always a thorn or two. My wife and I have attended all kinds of concerts, shows and plays during our marriage. We found out early on that this was something both of us thoroughly enjoyed. We have had season tickets for plays or concert series in Dayton, Cincinnati, and Oxford (Miami U.) and have attended numerous single shows in Dayton and Columbus as well as many other diverse places.

Ah, but the thorn, you ask? I never studied music in school. I was always better at the science side of things, so I graduated from college without ever playing an instrument of any kind. My musical talents seemed to lie in pushing the "ON" button or the purchasing of the ticket. After starting work and finding a number of friends who played various instruments I thought I would try something. I decided to try to learn to play the clarinet, since I greatly admired and enjoyed Pete Fountain, the jazz clarinetist. I took lessons on it for a few years and never really got much better than beginner. Lack of talent, lack of practice, lack of drive, who knows. I also found that the little finger on my left hand would lock up, which made it difficult to return it to position for the next note. Bummer! Obviously, the clarinet would not get me to Carnegie Hall, so I laid it aside.

A few years later my wife, a very good musician, bought me a guitar. It was an excellent guitar with very good tone. Once more into the game of lessons. I took individual lessons. I took group lessons. I could always reach beginner level. Progressing beyond that seemed to be the roadblock. It became obvious that the guitar would not take me to Carnegie Hall either.

I started taking lessons on the mountain dulcimer. I also took a few lessons from a local teacher from whom I bought the instrument, plus one all afternoon lesson from a really great dulcimer player. This was Maddie MacNiel, and the lesson was at the Black Swamp Dulcimer Festival, which is no longer held. At the end of that lesson I could play "Soldier Boy" reasonably well. Ah, but to play even the dulcimer you need to know more than one song. My next series of lessons on the dulcimer was in the University of Dayton Independent Learning in Retirement classes. The teacher for these classes had a method that made it easier to do the fingering of the frets. But this still requires practice, which I never did enough of. She was an excellent teacher, and I got farther along with the dulcimer than ever before. Obviously, this did not show up in class where I become a fumble fingered player.

A major part of this tragedy is that I have a great inability to remember more than five or six notes in a row. With almost all instruments, it is easier if you can remember notes. I figure that waiting until my early twenties to start on an instrument created the problem, although if I had musical talent I should have overcome that. The fact that I have always had more hobbies than time was probably also a critical factor. To play an instrument well requires a certain amount of diligence, which I probably have never really bitten the bullet on. Perhaps the kazoo. Ah well, enjoy the music. I pushed the "ON" button.

In the late seventies, I found the most enjoyable hobby I have ever had. My wife and I went to a local lake to watch a radio control sailboat regatta that had been mentioned in the paper. I asked a lot of questions, found out who made the fastest hulls and ordered one. This was a Marblehead class boat that is fifty inches long with a six-foot mast. It took me over a year to build it since I was on a learning curve while doing it. Over the years, I have had about 10 different RC boats, all sail. I currently own two that I race. I had finally found the most relaxing, most pressure-packed hobby anyone could have. It is relaxing when you are just out having fun, pressure-packed when you are in a race, particularly a national or regional championship. I have a large number of plaques and trophies attesting to the fact that I am good at it once in a while. Overall, I have won 28 trophy plaques over 26 years. These are all first, second or third place finishes in regattas that included club racing, away regattas, and regional regattas. I eventually became the National President of the organization and served in that post for three years, from 1994 to 1997. All of this I have to consider a major triumph.

Another personally satisfying triumph is getting into writing, mostly fictional short stories, but also some nonfictional things. It is an interesting process to sit down and put pen to paper as the saying goes. I write in many genres, but I usually try to fit in some humor. I think everything can be improved with a little humor. My fictional short stories range from flash fiction, which is less than 500 words, to one story of greater than 7,000 words. I have done a journal of my life and put together three soft-bound volumes on our family history, concentrating on my father's accomplishments. In 1944/1945, he worked on a top-secret project. This was the proximity fuse and is one of the three things given credit for winning World War II. Before the proximity fuse, which basically was a miniature radar, a shell had to hit an enemy plane to bring it down. With the proximity fuse, the shell could bring down the plane if it got within roughly 50 feet of it. One of the volumes I wrote is in the permanent library at Indiana University. Then in November 2011, the ultimate goal was accomplished. My writing group put together an anthology of Christmas stories. I had two stories in it, and my wife had one. It is publish-on-demand, but it still is a triumph that leaves a great feeling.

The closest thing to a major tragedy in my life was probably avoided because I played tennis. One day in May of 2004 I was playing in my regular foursome. After four games, I had four of the classical indicators of a heart problem. These included cold sweat, shortness of breath, pain in left side of chest, and a tightness down the left arm. I quit playing immediately, drove home, and told my wife what happened. To put it politely, she threw my butt in the car and drove me to the Dayton Heart Hospital. A major factor in this is that my father died of a heart attack in 1989 at the age of 79, and my older brother died of a heart attack in 1984 at the age of 53. Our family tradition was creeping up on me. The next day I was given a stress test, which showed indication of a blockage problem. The second day a catheterization was performed, and significant blockage in three arteries was found. The third day I had triple bypass surgery. Three days later, I was released from the hospital to go home with strict instructions about what I could and could not do. Thirty-four days later, my cardiologist said I could start playing tennis in another month. What could have been a major tragedy, even death, actually turned into a sort of triumph.

My biggest tragedy may be yet to come. Two doctors have told me it appears that about September 2010 I may have had a mini-stroke. With my family and medical history, e.g., high cholesterol problems, it is something that cannot be ruled out. The main result that triggered the doctor's decisions was the increase in two factors. I have always had some trouble remembering names, but now this has been accelerated. I can now forget a name within 24 hours. I almost never forget a face. It is just that I cannot always put a name with it. The longer time between seeing the person, the more certain that the name is gone from my memory. The second indicator that occurred very suddenly was not being able to remember how to get to places I had been going to for years. Restaurants, stores, people's homes being typical examples. All of these were impacted. If I had not been there within the last couple of weeks, I would need pointers from my wife. The directions part has improved measurably over the past two years, but the names part has not, so if I see you and say 'Hi' instead of 'Hi' plus your name, cut me some slack. Be glad I remembered your face.

My bucket list has become very moderate, with the prime item in it being to live longer than my father did. He lived to be 78 years, nine months, and 15 days old and died of heart failure. The second item in my bucket list is to not have a long painful death. With cholesterol/heart trouble, this is not usually a problem. A third item is, obviously, to enjoy the rest of my life, so stop bugging me. In the final measure, the quality of a person's life can be judged by the triumphs and tragedies they have encountered during their life. I think that my life goals were always to live reasonably well, take care of myself and my family and enjoy the heck out of life. I think I have accomplished that fairly well. I also think that my triumphs outweigh my tragedies. I can only emphasize the necessity of getting out there and enjoying life.

# THE GOLF GAME
## BY ROSE PEACOCK

Golf is a lot like the card game bridge. No one knows why you play it. Both of them are so stressful you vow to give them up forever each time you play. Then you are dealt a hand that you bid and make a grand slam. Or in the case of golf you make that perfect shot that makes you say "Yeah," and you return again for another round.

Now, I am not a par golfer by any means, but I usually don't hold up play because of the persistent urging of my husband to play faster. One day we were playing Forest Hills, which is a par-three course and one that you do not see par golfers playing. On this particular day, we had the course pretty much to ourselves and expected to have a pleasant round of golf. But as we were leaving the second hole green, we noticed a group of teenagers had teed off on hole one. We thought we were far enough ahead that it wouldn't matter. We would still have a pleasant round of golf. Apparently, the teenagers didn't like women on a golf course and proceeded to make comments. This mode of play continued until the fifth hole where they caught up with us. Now this hole tees off from a cliff and the green is far, far below.

Well, I stepped up to the tee, took careful aim and made my shot. That little ball took off, sailed into the air and over the cliff landing on the green about one inch from the hole. My young fellow golfers were needlessly impressed and did not have any more comments about women golfers the rest of the round.

*This story is based in truth. The author's hostess, Mika, on a recent trip to Czech Republic, told her about a man the age of her grandfather who was found, as a baby, in a basket on the church steps. "We don't know anything about his background," she explained, "but we know he was a good man who made his mark on the village he called home."*

# BABY IN THE BASKET
## BY MARY LOU MCCARTHY

*Czechoslovakia circa 1900*

Father Tomas heard a faint noise as he read the paper and sipped his breakfast tea. The aroma of Anna's chicken soup wafted in from the kitchen of the parish house. It was early morning, and he heard the sounds of the villagers farming in the fields or working in the square.

Anna was bustling around the kitchen, starting the noon meal, but the noise didn't come from the kitchen. It sounded like a cat meowing. Father Tomas dropped his paper and set out to investigate.

He hobbled to open the front door of the parish house, wincing at his sore toe from yesterday's impromptu football game in the street. There he found a basket, and gently removing the blanket, he found a baby boy.

By the way the infant was kicking and crying, Father Tomas guessed he was hungry. The good priest took the baby to Alzbeta's cottage—she was a new mother with a big family and a good heart.

As he walked through the village, he thought of the thousand souls who traced their family roots here for many generations. They were Roman Catholic for the most part, but there was a smattering of Lutherans and Episcopalians, and some souls whose religious disposition was known only to God.

Alzbeta's cottage was surrounded by a small flower garden in front, vegetables and fruit trees in back, a pen for the pig, a roost for ducks and chickens, and a small house for the guard dog. Father Tomas smiled as he opened the gate—the place certainly was full of life.

As he walked up to the house, he heard a ruckus from inside the cottage. Alzbeta and Jan had seven children, including a newborn. Father Tomas hoped there would be room for one more.

Alzbeta answered the door wearing a cheerful smile, tossed hair, and a spotted apron over her simple linen blouse and voluminous black skirt.

"Well, good morning, Father Tom, please come in!" she said. Children were popping out from the back of her skirt, from under the bed and, well, from everywhere.

"What do you have here—some fresh bread?" asked Alzbeta as she peeked in the basket. She stopped her bustling for a second and exclaimed, "OH, it's a baby!"

"Yes, a little boy," said Father Tomas. "That's why I'm here. I found this poor little fellow on the church steps this morning, and I immediately thought of you. Can you care for him, Alzbeta?"

"Of course, what's one more?" she laughed. "Don't forget what we say, Father, a guest is a gift from God."

"It will only be temporary," added Father Tom. "I will speak with the council to decide what to do."

He blessed all in the house and headed straight on to speak with Mojmir, the head of the village council.

"What, an infant on the church steps?" said Mojmir. "As if the drought and the sick milk cow weren't enough! Surely, God is laughing."

"God sent this baby to us," reminded Father Tom. "The boy came from this village, and he belongs in this village."

52

"Then the village will raise him," Mojmir nodded. "Each family will care for him for one month. I will make this recommendation to the council."

And so it was. They called him Little Josef Stepper, Josef for the head of the Holy Family, and Stepper for being found on the church steps.

With his small bag of clothes, Josef was moved from cottage to cottage on the first day of the month. He was treated as a member of each family and loved unconditionally. His birthday was celebrated on the day he was found at the church.

When Josef was eight, a farmer took him as a farm hand, in exchange for room and board. Joseph learned farming literally from the ground up, starting with mucking out the barns.

Farmer Peter told Josef that if the animals were cared for, the family would make it through the hard winter. They depended on the cows for milk, cream and butter, the chickens for eggs, the pigs for meat, and the goats for cheese.

Josef was lucky; he learned from the master farmer Maros, who was known throughout the village for his animal husbandry. Villagers sought his help when their stock encountered a problem.

One of Josef's first jobs was to collect eggs. A good chicken lays an egg a day, so in summer, they were overwhelmed with eggs.

Maros taught Josef how to put up eggs, saving them for the cold winter when the chickens did not produce. Josef had to carefully wash the eggs, then stand them up like soldiers, pointy side down, in a deep earthenware urn. When the bottom layer was completed, Maros mixed a slurry of lime and water and poured it over the eggs, then they layered eggs and slurry until the jar was filled. Maros then covered the urn with burlap, and placed it in the cold room under the cottage. "These eggs will take us through the winter," Peter stated.

When the snow came, it was Josef's job to get eggs for Marta. Come spring, the bottom of the jar was slimy and the eggshells were soft as he reached down to pick them up. Each day, Marta needed eggs for noodles and knedla (dumplings), kolach (sweets) and torta (cake), soup, and bread.

Josef grew and prospered. As a teenager, they said he had an empty leg to carry all the food he ate at dinner. But he just grinned and said he needed big nourishment to handle the big jobs—milking cows, feeding and caring for all the stock, planting, hoeing, watering and harvesting the grain, vegetables and fruit from the fields.

On baking day, Josef loaded the cart with the family's risen bread dough to be baked by the baker because his huge brick oven was much hotter than Marta's. To keep the bread separate, each mother marked her loaves with her family's initial. There was always an extra loaf marked with an "S" for Josef.

Josef grew stronger as Peter grew older and weaker, and they came to depend on each other. Josef admired Peter's wisdom, and Peter was grateful for Josef's strength.

Maros always called to Josef as he herded the stock into the barnyard pens, "Watch out for the bull. Each year Bruno gets worse—don't ever turn your back on that one."

Then one year, when Josef was 16, he was gored by the bull. Josef thought he herded Bruno safely inside the pen when suddenly, the bull turned, slashed out and hit Josef in his left eye, tearing his cornea and leaving him blind in one eye. Maros had Bruno slaughtered, regretting he waited one season too long.

One day when Josef was 20, word came from the neighboring village that a 16-year old girl was pregnant and looking for a husband. She would not divulge the father's name, and her actions heaped scandal on her family.

Sight unseen, Josef said, "I'll marry her." That simple statement changed his life forever.

They met and married the same day. Josef and Mariana had 12 children, all loved and cherished equally, including the one Mariana brought to the marriage.

The village was so grateful to Josef for marrying Mariana that they offered him a free cottage and the job as the village watchman for life.

After a long and happy life, both Josef and Mariana died in their small cottage, tended lovingly by their many children.

# THEN WHERE?

## BY MARIANNE WOESTE

She sits on the beach motionless
Mesmerized by the hypnotic rolling of ocean waves.
Her squinting eyes, following the sun's rays
Across the distant horizon, are vacant
Like the unrented summer cottage
Down the dirt road from her own.

Her wild, white hair shoots outward, like seaweed
And her weathered face bursts with freckles
Evidence of a coastal lifetime spent in sunshine.

Her husband's death has altered her life, she knows.
Her children tell her that she is alone now
That she doesn't remember the way she once did.
But they don't know about the wood storks
She remembers to feed
Or the sea turtles whose beachfront
She remembers to protect.

Why don't her children remember
That her home is with these waves?
Because if she isn't home here,
She wonders, then where?

# SOLVITUR AMBULANDO
## BY JUDY WHELLEY

I started having pain in my right hip. First just a twinge when I stood up, then a sharp pain when I walked, then it became a consistent ache. My first response was denial. This is not really a problem, just a little blip on the fitness radar. But it persisted to the point where I could see that my gait was changing as I favored that right hip, and I no longer wanted to walk.

I've never considered myself athletic. I was never on a competitive team, aside from cheerleading in high school. In my fifties, when my husband's betrayal surfaced, we began to walk together on the advice of a therapist. It was supposed to be a time to connect and to talk through some of the problems. It was meant to be healing. I needed something to dissipate the extreme angst, and walking helped me. I can't say it was healing for the relationship, but it was healing for me. When I first heard the phrase Solvitur Ambulando—attributed to Saint Augustine, it is Latin, for "It is solved by walking"—I resonated with the truth of it. I often cried as I walked, but I kept telling myself that for me the only way out is through. I would walk long enough for the endorphins to kick in and for clarity to surface.

I became a proficient walker, participating first in 5 and 10K's, then multiple half marathons and even one complete full marathon. One was enough! I realized that I did not want to devote the necessary time to be physically prepared to walk 26.2 miles, but walking remained an integral part of my life.

Now in my sixties, I have been examining beliefs I hold and questioning if they are true or simply ingrained old messages. One has to do with my body. I believed that if your body changed in some way, you had to accept and live with that change. So the possibility of having arthritis and no longer being able to count on my body to carry me through my healing, health-affirming, clarity-inducing walks was terrifying.

I decided to not acquiesce. I decided to try and walk through to the other side of the pain. My normal walking habit was three miles in the morning with an occasional second walk later in the day. Because of the hip pain, I had not walked much before leaving on a trip to Paris, a walker's paradise, but I did walk every day while there. These were not mapped out distance-walks but rather walks to get someplace. In Paris, all the "someplaces" were wonderful, so my motivation was high.

Upon returning home, I revisited Solvitur Ambulando. Another way of interpreting the phrase is "walk it off." I decided to start anew as a walker, to go back to the beginning. Our veterinarian suggested that my Yorkie, Buddy, needed more exercise, so I decided to walk one mile every day with Buddy. The first time I did it, I cried most of the way. It hurt. The second day, it hurt a little less. After about a week, it only hurt for the first half mile. After two weeks, I still felt discomfort but it was easily manageable. After three weeks, I realized that I had walked the mile pain free! Eureka!

So what have I learned? On the physical level, I learned I *can* change my body. I can make decisions and changes that impact my body in an affirmative way, that I am not separate from my body. On the thinking level, I learned I *can* change a belief. I can question whether something I have long held as a truth is accurate. And on an emotional level, I learned I *can* choose beliefs and actions that support my spiritual and physical growth and release those that don't.

I literally and figuratively walked through the pain and out the other side, refreshed and renewed.

Solvitur Ambulando.

# WAITING
## BY MARIAN SCHWILK-THOMAS

Someone has dressed her
   as for a day with friends,
   including well padded diapers.

She is old, very old, without a voice,
   strapped in a chair,
   busyness surrounds her.

She no longer cares.
   It is too late to reach for recovery,
   waiting for death to rescue her.

What was she in years past?
   Shy, aggressive, loving, hateful,
   confident, even passionate?

Oh the wars, disasters, inventions,
   a moon walk, the new millennium.
   She is a museum with shackled doors.

I would surround her with angels
   and spirits to console the soul
   that waits, waits and waits...

# LADY C

## BY WANDA BEAMER

Twenty-one year old Danny O'Brian was excited. He was about to begin his first day as a police officer for Keller City Police Department. The night before, he barely slept, driven to repeatedly polish his shoes and iron his new white shirt until he was certain it had enough starch in it to stand on its own. Yes, he was ready to begin his long awaited career as a policeman.

His assignment was to patrol Keller's Downtown Business District. Early in the morning as he turned to walk down Maple Street, he saw an elderly woman sitting on a grate on the snowed-covered sidewalk. There she sat in a tattered cape with her disheveled clothes piled around her.

It appeared as if she were patiently waiting for what little heat the grate would grudgingly allow to escape from the depths of the city. The midwinter snowflakes gently fell on the cold cement walk. Stoic and expressionless, she simply sat there, staring at nothing.

Officer O'Brian noticed her obliviousness to the day, place and time. The people passed by her, sometimes pausing for a moment before continuing on their way. The sight of a woman sitting on the cold sidewalk in the middle of winter, holding a small brown tattered book in her hand, as if she were in her own living room, may have shocked them. Maybe they had no idea of what to do or say, or maybe they were simply late. Regardless, each passerby had his or her reasons not to stop.

Officer O'Brian wondered what painful circumstances led her to the sidewalks of the busy downtown street. He was prepared to handle assaults, petty thefts and other criminal behavior. However, the sight of a fragile old woman, sitting on a grate with a tattered cape being the only protection she had between her and a half inch of snow, was not something they covered at the Police Academy.

He attempted to engage her in a conversation. The only response from her was a blink of her eyes, which also allowed the snow on her eyelashes to fall down on her cheeks. She looked resigned to dying right there. O'Brian contacted his captain before he called an Emergency Medical Team (EMT) to the scene.

The Captain and the EMT arrived at the same time, and the lady was taken to the nearest hospital. She died that evening from "unknown causes." The Captain took Officer O'Brian aside and explained how the lady became well known to the police department. She was "Lady C."

Her father was a well-established businessman, who made his fortune on Wall Street. Lady C's life started out as a fairy tale and she was the princess. Unfortunately, her life turned into a nightmare instead. She was well educated, spoke several languages and was well traveled. To all, it appeared the world was in her hands. That was until that fateful day she met the love of her life. Her father was against the marriage, but she married the man anyway, and her father disinherited her.

Her young husband was a charming failure but not much of a businessman. They were destined for hard times and acrimony. Soon, her only joy in life was her daughter. One day as they were driving through the city, Lady C and her husband began to argue. The more heated the argument became, the faster he drove. He swerved to miss an oncoming truck, rolling the car into a utility pole. Both he and her daughter died in the accident.

Since that day, Lady C did not speak a word. She was admitted to a series of hospitals, assigned social workers and eventually placed in group homes. She was supported as much as the system could allow. Not being a danger to others or herself, she was allowed a certain amount of freedom to go and come from the group home.

Yes, the accident happened within a block of where she sat. Looking upon her face, one might wonder what thoughts occupied her mind.

Just before the Captain returned to his office, he told Officer O'Brian the reason they called her Lady C. Apparently she carried an old leather photo album with an engraved letter C on the cover. The album contained pictures of her daughter named Carolyn.

Now, many years have passed since Officer O'Brian's first day on the job. He has never forgotten his image of Lady C sitting motionless in the snow. He thinks of her as an example of what a policeman knows about a small community he serves; life is fragile and unfair. The Police Academy prepared him for assaults, petty thefts and odd behavior, but not for life's varieties of anguish, which often prompts them. Each year on the anniversary of the beginning of his career, he makes a point to walk down Maple Street, stop at the grate and maintain a moment of silence in her memory.

*The following story is from Der Wunschmeister, a book of short stories by the author about an antique shop with hundreds of seemingly useless items for sale by a mysterious jinn. The items have the magical powers to fulfill your dreams at often frightening prices. The narrator is an unwilling servant of the jinn.*

# THE SCRAPBOOK
## BY DON HART

I had a difficult time wresting the scrapbook from the dead woman. She had clutched it tightly to her breast as she died. And I must say, there are probably very few deaths on this troubled planet more beautiful than the death of Ann Winning. She died looking so very pleased, filled with lovely memories of a happy and productive life.

It was Malaniel, the proprietor of the Antique Shoppe to whom I am indentured, who sent me to retrieve the scrapbook.

I had to sit with her for over two hours before her death, and she talked the entire time, excepting for the last five minutes or so. She told me of a cherished Uncle Claude from Santa Fe who left her a fortune, giving her thousands of exquisite possessions and allowing her the freedom to love her life completely. His greatest legacy, however, was his total devotion to his niece and a superb philosophy he taught her.

Bequeathed with a worldly fortune and a wise philosophy to enjoy it, she told me how she devoted her time to her only son and his wonderful family. How she loved working on behalf of unhappy orphans and stray animals. I was especially enthralled by her elaborate descriptions of exciting cities where she had traveled, and of warm friendships she made with strange people from far off places, and how she managed to keep lively communications open with them for many years.

I was moved by her deteriorating zest, using her dying words to give thanks to God for her life, a life filled with beautiful gardens, memorable loves and great cuisine enjoyed all over the world. She seemed beatific as she described so many happy events, almost as though she had one foot in heaven already.

Her life seemed to have been filled with only Saturdays, Sundays and terrific holidays complete with good laughter, anticipation of good things to come and exuberant love for every contented moment of fun and excitement.

Her professional and athletic achievements were discussed in a frank manner, not boastful, but portrayed with an assurance that rang true. These accomplishments had the sound of authenticity and were detailed to tell events minutely. She explained how her careful prior efforts and good preparations were always the prelude to fine results.

I envied her most in the way she talked about her family. They were her most prized memory. Her son, Michael, was her total joy. And, he had four children, all of them an endless source of happiness to Ann: twin granddaughters and two fine boys after them had pleased her forever with their wit and remarkable deeds.

It was a pity someone so joyous had to die, but God had set her clock from the beginning of time, and now was the hour she would be taken. Malaniel told me the day before that she would pass away at 4:16 PM. He has the ability to forecast the time that Death will take someone, that is, someone with whom he has done business.

"Be there early to retrieve the gray scrapbook, and get out of there as soon as possible. If you keep her talking, her vital signs will stay up, and she will get extra hospital attention. If they come to her rescue it will make it harder for you to get back the book," Malaniel said.

"But what if her family is there? Won't they protect the book, knowing how dear it is to her?"

"I have made arrangements so that they will not be there," Malaniel said firmly.

On my return to the Antique Shoppe, I stopped to look inside the large scrapbook. All the pages were blank. Just smooth white paper with no pictures or letters attached. The outside was gray and embossed with the words 'Wonderful Memories.' There were no entries anywhere in the book, even though Ann Winning had referred to various pages when she told me of 'events of her long life.'

The truth, I later learned, was that Ann did not live a very long life. She was not much more than 50 years old a few months before I watched her die in the hospital. When I came for the book, she remembered seeing me with Malaniel at the Antique Shoppe. She would not return the scrapbook, she said, under any conditions.

Before she told me some of the memories of a wonderful life, she asked me if I were an angel. I told her I was not.

"Then, perhaps Malaniel is an angel," she said. "Do you know if he is a good angel or a fallen one?" she asked me.

"I do not know what Malaniel is," I told her, "but he and his business are extraordinary. I only follow his wishes. I can do nothing else."

"Then you'd best be careful what you wish for, especially when handling the items in his shop," she said.

These things I already knew. They were the source of my anguish since long ago when I first stepped into his Antique Shoppe and told him my fervent wish.

Ann had fabricated most of the stories she told me before she died. She certainly had no fortune, had probably never traveled and the professional and athletic accomplishments she detailed were most likely untrue. I even doubted she had a son named Michael or grandchildren. The previous times I had seen her at the

Antique Shoppe, she was little more than a bag lady. She was, however, a very loving and cheerful person.

I considered keeping the book and saving it for my last wish, but I could never get away with betraying Malaniel.

I returned it to the Shoppe, "Here is the scrapbook from Ann Winning."

"Did you have any difficulties?" Malaniel asked.

"No, except that she would not give it up until after she died, and even then her clutch was very strong."

He took the book in a grateful manner and said, "You will be rewarded 25 for this."

I was pleased to have this 25 to spend alone and away from the Antique Shoppe and from Malaniel's terrible mysteries. I was not sure if the 25 was granted as a vacation only, or if 25 days were to be added to my lifetime.

"You may also go for another 25, if you wish, after Ann Winning's son Michael visits the shop."

"Then, she did have a son. Has he told you he is coming?"

"No, but I expect him in a few days. He will try to purchase a scrapbook like the one his mother bought for 10,000. He will want to buy one for money. Be careful not to talk while he is here, unless I ask you a question."

Malaniel's prediction was right. Toward the end of the week, we were visited in the Antique Shoppe by a young Michael Winning. He was a tall man of about 30 years with a most pleasant manner. As instructed, without a word, I took him directly to see Malaniel.

"I am the son of Ann Winning, one of your customers," Michael announced.

"Yes, may I be of service?"

"My mother passed away several days ago," he said.

"I have heard of it," Malaniel said, "and I give you my sympathy. She was truly a lovely person."

"Yes, she was," said Michael, "And the dearest person I shall ever know. But I wonder if perhaps you have another scrapbook like the one you sold her a few months back, before she got sick."

"I have no other quite like it, I am sorry to say, but perhaps you will look around my shop and find something else. Tell me, what is your most fervent wish?"

Michael seemed startled by the question. He said that the only wish he had was to see his mother again. He told us she was only 49 years old and had been in the best of health, but suddenly lost both physical and mental well being. As her body became ravaged with an unknown disease, she also became mentally unbalanced and spoke of her lost uncle and all sorts of wonderful events that never happened. She seemed even more happy than before her health went bad, but her fantasies became larger and more embellished.

"All she wanted to do was talk about unbelievable memories and show me imaginary pictures she said she saw in the scrapbook."

"What did she show you?" asked Malaniel.

"Just blank pages."

"Did she tell you anything else?"

"No. Just that she had purchased the scrapbook from you for a very high price, something like ten thousand! And she used it to make a wish. And the wish was coming true."

"What did she say was her wish?" Malaniel asked.

"She told me she wished for 'wonderful memories for her and her family,' but I am her only family. I have a new wife, but that's all. She made up stories about me having four children. And Mother certainly had no money to pay you thousands of dollars for a scrapbook, did she? She worked as a house cleaner when she could find any work. I always gave her money."

"She paid me no money for the book," Malaniel assured him.

"Well, the book she loved is lost now, and I had hoped you would have another one like it. That book made her so completely happy, even while she was dying. I would like to find one like it as a keepsake."

"I am sorry, Mr. Winning, I have no other like it. Is there something else you might want? Tell me, what is your fervent wish?"

"I really miss my mother. It's all so odd. Some of Mother's fantasy wishes might be coming true," Michael said. "I just learned this morning that my wife is pregnant with twins. That was one of the fantasies Mother had. That I had twin daughters and other children. She talked like it was already true."

"Perhaps it was always meant to be true," Malaniel said softly. "Has anything else come true?"

"No, pretty much the opposite," Michael chuckled. "We received a telegram from Santa Fe that my Great Uncle Claude also passed away and his funeral bill needs paid. I don't think he had any money, though. But I don't know anything about him, except that Mother always loved him and had good wishes for him, even after he disappeared years ago."

"Did she tell you she loved your uncle before she got sick?" asked Malaniel.

"Of course, why wouldn't she? She loved pretty much everyone."

As Michael left the shop with shoulders slumped, I had to wonder if Ann's wonderful memories and happy death were truly worth the 10,000 to her; after all, that's more than 27 years.

# THE JOURNEY
## BY BOB MACKENZIE

"Alice, do you think I'm going away?"

Alice's body tensed as she stood at the sink washing dishes. She didn't like conversations that started with that sort of question. Ever since their marriage, 42 years ago, it made her tense and the hairs on the back of her neck stand up. Her thumb inadvertently slid across the clean plate she was holding, emitting an audible squeak.

"What do you mean going away, Ted?"

"You know, like not being here, like not being who I was." Ted had been wondering about this for some time. "You know, a person grows older and suddenly something takes over and—you don't know anymore."

"Don't know what anymore, Ted?"

"Oh, shit, Alice, you know, like am I still me?"

Alice frowned, and then thought, "Something is different about this conversation. Is Ted facing some crisis?" She left the sink, wiping her hands on her flowered apron, and went over to the table to sit in a chair opposite him.

"Ted, what's going on? Is there something you've been keeping from me? Are you ill? Have you been to the doctor?"

"No, nothing like that." Alice and Ted had had a good life together. They raised three successful children, gone on numerous vacations together, shared a love of gardening, and worked hard to keep a happy home, but now something was looming for Ted that even he didn't understand.

"I just seem to be having some problems or thoughts lately that I find disturbing."

Not knowing where to go with this, Alice said, "What specifically are you talking about?"

"You know, I forget things. The calendar is a nightmare for me; I have no idea when we're doing what, and I'm having trouble remembering names. I'm afraid I'm going away."

Alice shuddered at the implication of Ted's words. Could he just be overly worried, or was he really "going away?"

"Ted, I'm your wife, and I really can't say that I've noticed any remarkable difference in you in the last few months. What the hell has gotten into you?"

"Hell, hell, what do you know about hell? When I run across what's his name on the street and I can't pull that name out of my head, that's hell! If you looked up embarrassing in the dictionary; that's about it!! When that happens, I just shrivel up and wish I could croak."

"Whoa, Ted, I think you're overreacting. We all have trouble remembering names and things, but it doesn't mean we're losing it or 'going away.' Why are you so worried?"

"Dammit Alice, you don't understand. If I'm going away, I'm not so much concerned about me, I'm concerned about you."

"Ted, don't be concerned about me, I'm a big girl. I can take care of myself."

"Big talk, Alice. Can you take care of the finances? Do you know where our money is invested? Have you taken any responsibility for understanding our allocation ratio between stocks and bonds? If it comes to the point where I can't manage the finances anymore, will you be able to live on for years without my help?"

"Jeez, Ted, you're talking like you're going to die tomorrow. You're still in good health, and as long as you're well, what do I need to know? You've managed this stuff on your own all this time, why should it change now?"

"This is why I hate these conversations, Alice, you just don't get it. If you go into a nursing home, I know how I'll proceed with our resources to keep you being stuck in a hellhole. Can you say the same, if I get disabled?"

"Ted. Ted, you're not going to get disabled. You're my old reliable."

"God dammit, Alice, I'm getting aggravated! When will you come to grips with the fact that you can't predict the future, and you have no idea in hell what's going to happen today, let alone tomorrow?"

"Ted, you're getting aggressive and you're scaring me. Please, I don't need to hear anymore. Why don't you lie down in the den while I finish the dishes and I'll join you? We can talk about it more then."

"That's right, Alice, avoid the issue and make believe there's nothing to worry about! I hoped and keep hoping that someday you'll take responsibility and you'd let me teach you about our finances. But, no, you just want to go along in your happy little world believing that nothing bad will ever happen. Alice, I hate to say it, but you are stupid!"

"Get the hell out of here! Go in the den, lie down, and watch TV. You are really upsetting me, and I don't want to talk to you anymore! Go!"

"Screw it, I'm going. It's impossible to talk to you about a serious subject. Fine, I'm going. Damn!"

Ted walked into the den, snapped the TV on to a football game and lay down on the couch. He thought about how he might get Alice to take his questions seriously. He concluded: it would never happen. He closed his eyes and began to enter the peaceful realm of sleep.

Alice stood over the sink, furious at Ted for challenging her to take on responsibility for something he was so good at. Her mind was racing, trying to come up with a good response for Ted. Then it hit her, I'll tell Ted, "I've watched you change a tire several times, but I still can't change a tire. If I ever need to, change a tire, I'll learn how." After all, isn't that what life's all about? You get thrown into the mêlée and you learn to swim. What's the big deal?

That's it, she thought, I'll finish these dishes and tell Ted. The weight was lifted; Alice began to feel better now that she had a comeback. It made her smile and before she knew it, the dishes were done. She wiped her hands on the towel at the sink and walked toward the den.

"Ted, I want to tell you what I've been thinking about what you were saying."

Ted didn't answer.

"Ted, did you fall asleep? I'm sorry, the conversation got out of hand, but I've been thinking and I want to tell you something."

Ted did not answer.

"God dammit, Ted, I know you're not happy with me, but don't ignore me; I hate that!"

Ted did not answer.

Alice walked closer to the couch and touched Ted on the shoulder. He didn't respond. It was then that Alice realized Ted had gone away.

The coroner said it was a massive cerebral hemorrhage that took him. Alice could only wonder if Ted had a premonition. How could it be that he was healthy one day and dead the next?

So many preparations for his funeral, so much to do. Soon Alice began to worry about the bills; there was little money in the checking account. She felt some relief in remembering that Ted had always provided for emergencies with his investments. Then it hit her hard: she could no longer ask anything of Ted.

Ted had gone away.

# PATTI'S SONG
## BY D. A. QUIGLEY

I made my way past the nurse who was busy monitoring Patti's vitals. First I sat in the corner out of the way. Then I went to check my wife. Staring into her eyes as she lay on a hospital gurney in the busy emergency room was very scary. Her eyes told the whole story of her condition…it was critical. The sounds and actions of doctors and nurses caused uneasy tensions in my brain. Loudspeakers were broadcasting coded messages, causing nurses and specialists to sprint from one location to another at some new alarm.

I tried to tell her that she would be alright. The walls of the room were made of a light green fabric and provided a small amount of privacy. My wife lay on a metal gurney covered with a black pad about an inch thick. Two new nurses were busy attaching IV strips. It had only been 36 hours since she had come home from the hospital. She had been happy at home after 14 days of surgery and rehab. Now she was back.

Our non-verbal communication was interrupted by the surgeon in charge of my wife's care.

"Mr. Quigley, you will have to leave now. I need to perform a procedure," said the doctor. He was dressed in a surgical gown and a hooded hat. He looked like he was treating a HAZMAT site.

"How serious is her condition?" I asked.

"She is a very sick woman…She might not make it." The chaplain for the hospital was standing close by as he spoke.

November 8th would become a date when a new door in our life together would open. It was the day my wife entered the hospital for surgery on her spine. She had suffered for years with severe back pain, the effects of a broken steel rod that was fused to her spine in the mid 1980's. As the years passed, the broken rod caused her to lose lung capacity, more frequently requiring a cane to walk, as she grew shorter in height. The disease is more commonly referred to as "curvature of the spine." During the last forty years, this would be her third surgical operation to correct this condition. The first one took place when she was nineteen.

This operation was to have been two procedures in one day only separated by a few hours. Because of the length of her first procedure, which required more time than planned, the doctors did not risk beginning a second operation that day. The delay should have been a clue to me of what lay ahead. Sure enough, a day later, the doctors discovered a blood clot in her right leg, which prompted all sorts of additional tests and procedures.

Nine days later, she had her second operation to replace the broken rod with two longer ones. This operation was supposed to allow her to stand more upright and gain height. This procedure went well and after spending Thanksgiving in the hospital she was discharged to go home on the Saturday after Thanksgiving. We really looked forward to this opportunity to share a meal together and get some much needed sleep in our own bed.

The next day started mysteriously for Patti. She was not herself. After skipping breakfast, she spent the rest of the morning in her bed trying to get rest. She began to get feverish and hallucinate. She also had lost strength and had difficulty navigating even short distances. Our children who had come to see her for breakfast started to become concerned.

Our visiting nurse was scheduled to arrive at 4 PM but called in sick and another nurse had to fill in. The substitute came to the house earlier than expected. Upon her arrival, she noticed the seriousness of my wife's condition and had me call the surgeon immediately who recommended we call an ambulance. In less than 24 hours, my wife was returning back to the same hospital where she had been discharged the day before. Her temperature was 103 degrees and her blood pressure was only 57. She was basically non-responsive.

After securing the house, I followed the ambulance to the hospital. I thought it was strange the crew did not have emergency lights on. It gave me a false sense of hope about her condition. Being alone in the car made me think of the different possibilities for the cause of her illness.

I remembered the eyes of the substitute nurse who checked my wife at home. My memory of how they looked sent a message of fear and concern. I was very thankful for that nurse coming to our home when she did. I did not know it at the time, but she saved Patti's life that afternoon.

Changing the radio dial, I found a station playing pop country music. I quickly recognized a song that Patti and I heard weeks before. We had made it our personal favorite. Little did I know that this song and its lyrics would be repeated in my brain many times over in the next weeks and months..."I'm Gonna Love You Though It."

When I arrived at the hospital, I followed the crew to the Emergency Area. The whole scene in the emergency room seemed surreal; actions moved in slow motion, even though the medics were reacting to my wife's condition as fast as they could. Two nurses got busy trying to monitor Patti's vitals and elevate her blood pressure with IVs. All were trying to determine what was causing the infection ravishing her body. The look in her glassy eyes made my mind race through many memories of our 47 years of marriage.

I held her hand and whispered the title of a song, *I'm Gonna Love You Through It*, made famous by Martina McBride. Little did we know when we first heard these lyrics, "I am going to love you through it" would become a powerful message of hope. I kept hearing the words of the song as they were playing in the back of my mind: When you're frail, I'll be strong; when you quit, I'll hold on.

My sons and I would spend the next few hours with family members who had arrived concerned with her relapse. It would be a long night. The next 24 hours seemed like a blur. After being stabilized, she was transferred to Intensive Care. We waited a long time to get some word on what was causing her condition.

The next day brought us the answer. She had contracted MRSA (methicillin-resistant Staphylococcus aureus), a nasty bacterium often contracted in hospitals, deadly and hard to treat. To find the source of the disease, our surgeon performed a procedure in the operating room the previous night. He was assisted by a plastic surgeon who specialized in the treatment of critical wounds. They discovered the source of the disease and removed a great deal of tissue and muscle from her lower back. The doctors would later describe her back incision as the "Grand Canyon of incisions." The cut now was sealed with an instrument called a "wound vac." A small pump attached to the wound helped keep the disease from spreading and destroying more tissue. Patti was then transferred to a new residence in the hospital: The Burn Unit. The whole episode terrified me. She would spend the next 60 days in the Burn Unit. Her recovery was just beginning, but there would be many more challenges that she faced on a daily basis.

Her story is not one of tragedy or triumph in a classic sense. Patti faced many hardships during a four-month hospital stay and home therapy thereafter. The power of many prayers and well wishes from friends and family helped her get to where she is today. Progress is a measure in your mind, not necessarily in days and actions. It requires a positive attitude in order to have a chance of succeeding.

My wife is a very strong person. Her strong will and determination are what has made our family successful. The tragedy we faced is part of our love story, which made our relationship stronger. I realized what was important in my life, and I dedicated myself to helping her through the new challenges that occurred when we opened that door in November.

I attended a concert with my son this past summer (a Father's Day present). The artist who headlined the performance just happened to be Martina McBride. She sang her memorable song that night: *I'm Gonna Love You Through It.*

All the emotions and memories of those agonizing months were captured in a few short minutes that hot summer night when I heard those lyrics again at this concert. I find myself often thinking about this song and how it changed our lives. Songs, poems and stories can be very powerful in how they help us cope. Many times they provide healing powers not felt at the time, but there nonetheless.

Also by University of Dayton Writers' Group:

*Anthology of Christmas Memories*
Edited by Don Hart and Bob Mackenzie
Introduction by Nancy Pinard

List Price: $10.95

ISBN-13: 978-0615570907
ISBN-10: 0615570909

This anthology is a whimsical collection of short stories, memoirs and poems written by 16 seniors, nearly all in their 70s, spanning holidays from 1930-2011. The authors are from southwestern Ohio and meet at the University of Dayton's Lifelong Learning Institute. Stories are about "what it's really like to play Santa," how a child perceives the mysteries of Christmas, and the tortuous adult worries and last minute pressures of holidays. Memories of the Great Depression, World War II and the entanglements of recent years are woven into these tales. You'll read about a Santa who robs a bank, a boy in a monastery, adults having faith restored and the timelessness of love. Some of the stories are meant to be read aloud to children. There's even a great recipe. This book makes a memorable gift to be unpacked yearly with your Christmas decorations.

www.ingramcontent.com/pod-product-compliance
Lightning Source LLC
Chambersburg PA
CBHW071411170626
46811CB00003B/1357